THE IN-BETWEEN BOOK

CHRISTOPHER WILLARD * OLIVIA WEISSER
* *Art by* ALISON OLIVER

sounds true
BOULDER, COLORADO

Have you ever noticed that there is a space between everything? There is space between you and other people, between pictures on the wall, between notes in a song. You might think these spaces are empty, but they actually help us see the shape and beauty of everything around us in a whole new way—even in ways that some grown-ups cannot see. This book will show you how to mindfully notice these spaces and become more curious, calm, and creative.

Close your eyes. That's a weird thing to do while reading a book! Now focus on your body. Can you find the teeny, tiny pause between breathing in and breathing out? Focusing on this space can help you feel more relaxed.

If you are reading this book with someone else, rest your head on their chest. If you are reading this book by yourself, put your hand on your own chest. Listen or feel for heartbeats. Are there spaces between them?

Trace the space between these flowers with your finger. What shape does it make? Can you trace the space between other objects around you? Between the trees on your street? Between the toys in your room?

Stand up and take a few steps around the room. Is there a moment of stillness when one footstep turns into the other?

What about the pause between
jumping up and coming back down?

Now look out the window. What can you see between the clouds?

If it's nighttime, what can you see in the space between the stars or the lights in your neighborhood?

Slowly sit back down and notice just when your body touches the surface underneath you. Can you feel the moment in between standing and sitting?

Now make your body as quiet as possible, maybe even closing your eyes again, and listen to all the sounds around you. What do you hear between the sounds? Is there actually any silence?

Tell a joke to a parent or a friend. Do you notice a pause between your joke and their laugh?

Can you think of any other in-between spaces? What about the pause between a question and an answer? Try to find that pause as you read one of the questions in this book. If you are thinking about an important question, and you stop to listen, does it help you find the answer you are looking for?

Turn to the person reading this book with you and give them a hug. Can you feel a space between you? What are the feelings between you?

Clap your hands.

Focus on the space
between claps.

Can you find anything hidden in the spaces between these lines? For an extra challenge: What did you feel in the time between looking at this picture for the first time and discovering something hidden within it?

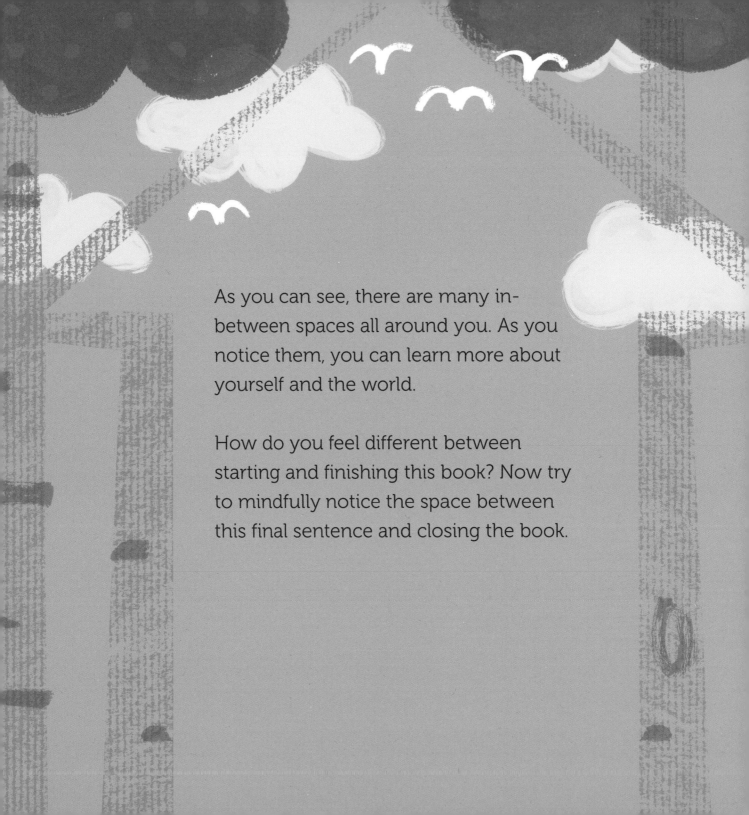

As you can see, there are many in-between spaces all around you. As you notice them, you can learn more about yourself and the world.

How do you feel different between starting and finishing this book? Now try to mindfully notice the space between this final sentence and closing the book.

This book was inspired by the Japanese idea of *ma*. Ma is the space between everything. It can be the space between people, time, sounds, and more. That empty space helps us notice the things around it. And that space is important because it connects everything. It allows you to see yourself and the world in new ways.

Many creative people know about ma. An artist knows how to draw things, as well as the shapes of spaces between things. This is called "negative space." A poet leaves space between words to make the words stand out. A musician knows that silences within the music make a performance great. Athletes watch the space between players, the ball, and the goal. Good friends know how to be quiet and listen. And wise people know the secret that there is space between our thoughts and feelings. And now you know, too.

Where else can you find the in-between spaces? What do you think you might discover there?

間

To Mae and Leo
—CW and OW

For Nina
—AO

Sounds True
Boulder, CO 80306

Published 2021

Book design by Ranée Kahler
Cover illustration by Alison Oliver

Printed in South Korea

Library of Congress Cataloging-in-Publication Data

Names: Willard, Christopher (Psychologist), author. | Weisser, Olivia,
  author. | Oliver, Alison, illustrator.
Title: The in-between book / Christopher Willard and Olivia Weisser ; art
  by Alison Oliver.
Description: Boulder, CO : Sounds True, 2021. | Audience: Ages 4-8. |
  Summary: "An interactive book about the Japanese concept of "ma," or the
  space between things, helps children learn about mindfulness"-- Provided
  by publisher.
Identifiers: LCCN 2020038185 (print) | LCCN 2020038186 (ebook) |
  ISBN 9781683647331 (hardback) | ISBN 9781683647348 (ebook)
Subjects: LCSH: Mindfulness (Psychology)--Juvenile literature.
Classification: LCC BF637.M56 W55 2021 (print) | LCC BF637.M56 (ebook) |
  DDC 158.1/3--dc23
LC record available at https://lccn.loc.gov/2020038185
LC ebook record available at https://lccn.loc.gov/2020038186

10 9 8 7 6 5 4 3 2 1